IS FOR
IMMIGRANTS

Selina Alko

Christy Ottaviano Books

Henry Holt and Company
New York

Ancestors

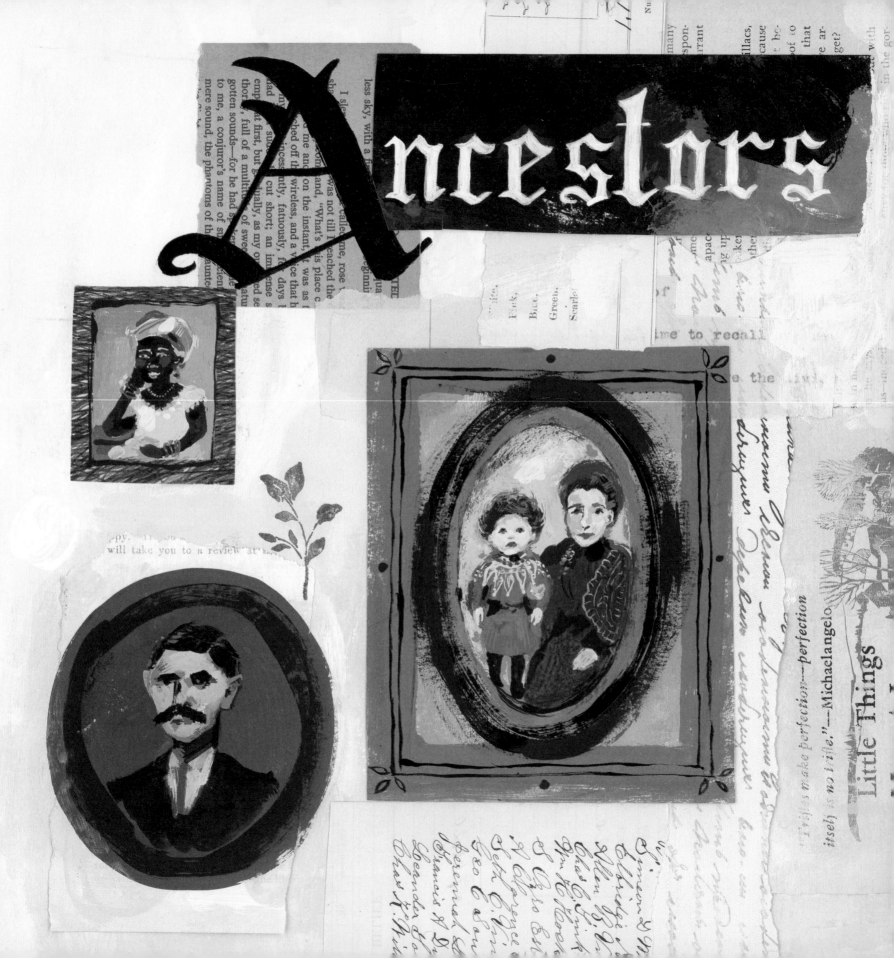

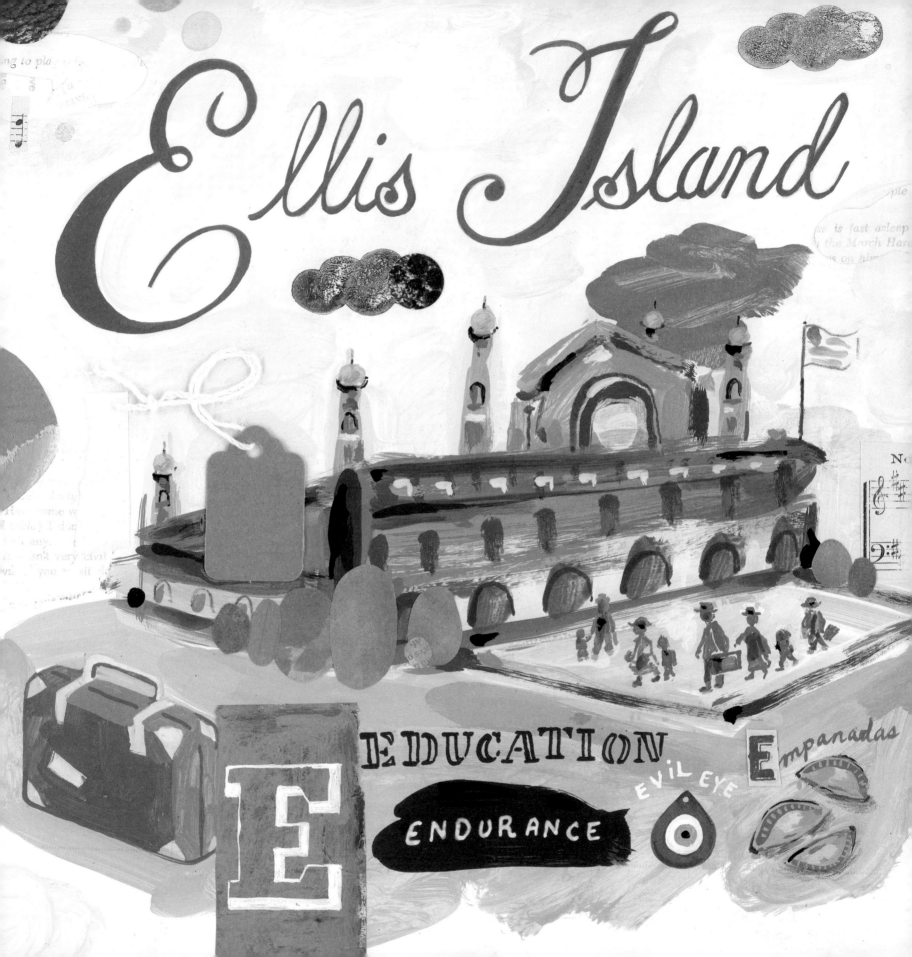

HERITAGE

H

HOLiDAYS

HANUKKAH

HiTabs

holi

HOPE

ILLUSTRATION BY WES DUVALL

Kabuki

kimchi

KIND-
NESS

KIELBASA

MOSQUES

M

MOTHERS Martial arts

MOROCCAN TILES

MOSAICS

VIETNAMESE SANDWICHES (BANH MI)

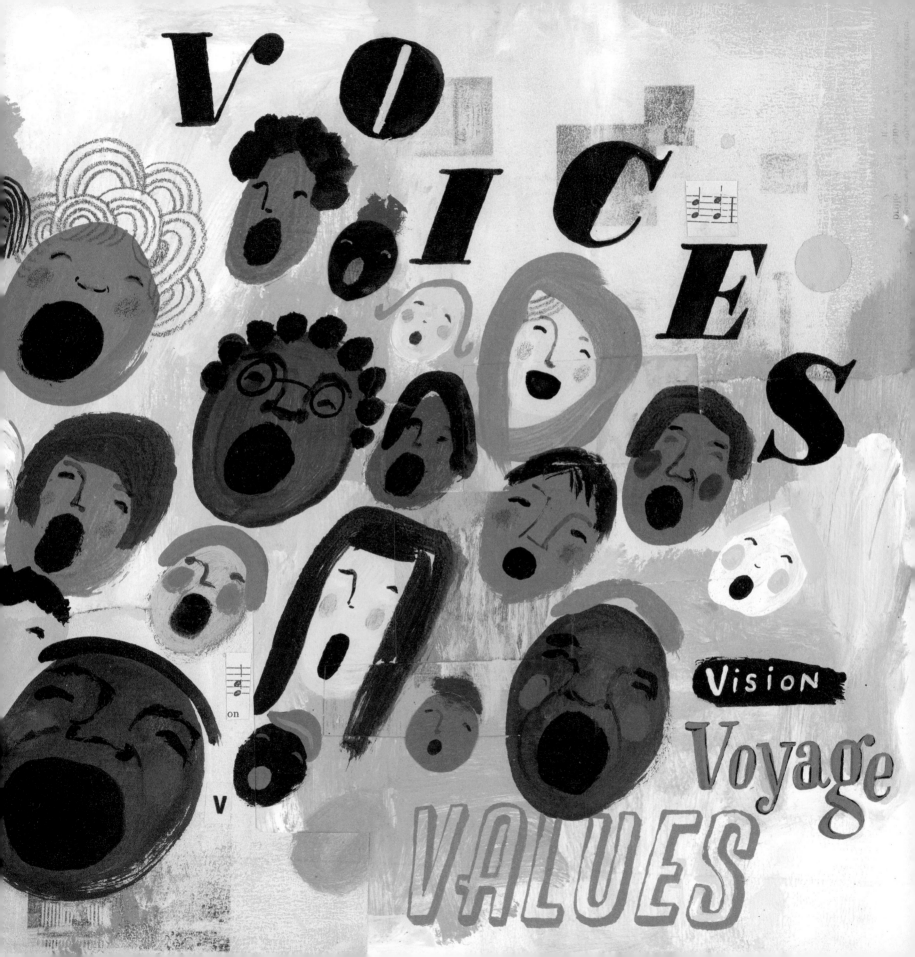

X

XYLOPHONE

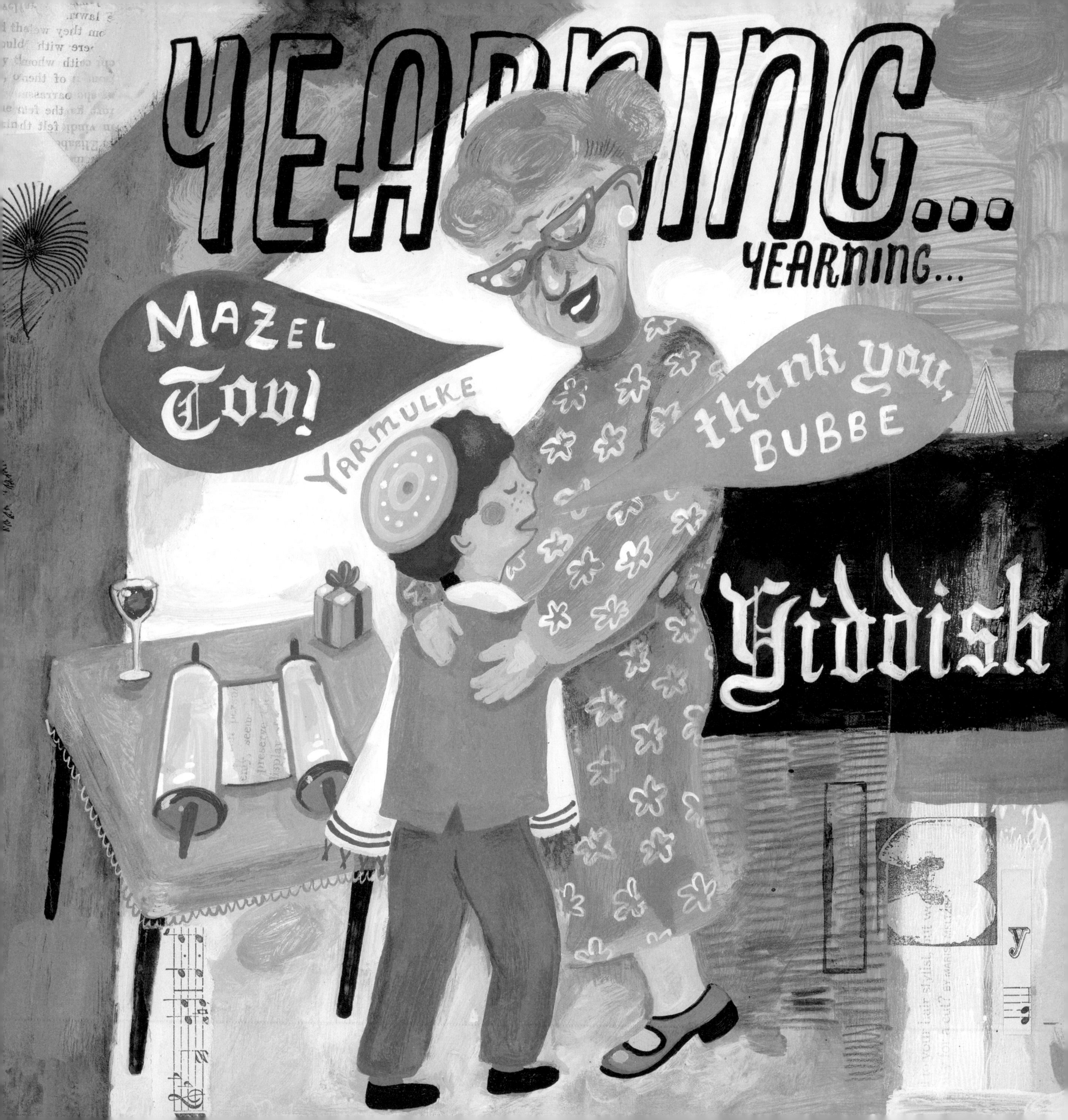
YEARNING...
MAZEL Tov!
YARMULKE
thank you, BUBBE
Yiddish
13
y

Zz

Zest

Ziti dinner

To my remarkable father, Henri Alko (born Henri Aaron Albukrek),
who spoke seven languages and taught me how to paint.

And special thanks to Emily Nussbaum for her wise input on the project.

Author's Note

There is so much that is wonderful about our diverse American culture—from bodegas and food trucks to martial arts and Turkish delight. America is a nation of immigrants. People immigrate to America for all sorts of reasons: sometimes in search of adventure or education, sometimes fleeing violence or poverty. There are eager immigrants and there are refugees seeking a safe haven. There are also descendants of African slaves, who were brought to America against their will through brutal means. America isn't any one thing; it's many, and each family has its own distinct experience.

The topic of immigration is close to my heart. I grew up with a first-generation Turkish Jewish father and a second-generation Eastern European Jewish mother in British Columbia, Canada. As an adult, I moved to the United States to attend art school in New York City. Little did I know how intensely I would yearn to stay—that pursuing a career in children's books would become a dream I would work endlessly to achieve. I am happy to say that I became an American ten years ago and have raised my family in this magnificent and complex country that I now call my own.

Henry Holt and Company, *Publishers since 1866* • Henry Holt® is a registered trademark of Macmillan Publishing Group, LLC.
120 Broadway, New York, New York 10271 • mackids.com • Copyright © 2021 by Selina Alko. All rights reserved.
Library of Congress Cataloging-in-Publication Data is available • Our books may be purchased in bulk for promotional, educational, or business use.
Please contact your local bookseller or the Macmillan Corporate and Premium Sales Department at (800) 221-7945 ext. 5442 or by email at
MacmillanSpecialMarkets@macmillan.com. • First Edition, 2021 • Gouache and collage on Arches watercolor paper were used to create
the illustrations for this book. • Printed in China by RR Donnelley Asia Printing Solutions Ltd., Dongguan City, Guangdong Province.
ISBN 978-1-250-23786-6
1 3 5 7 9 10 8 6 4 2